1/10

D0014336

P7 - AST - 092

Stinky

By

Dave and Pat Sargent

Illustrated by
Jane Lenoir

Ozark Publishing, Inc.
P.O. Box 228
Prairie Grove, AR 72753

Sargent, Dave, 1941-
    Stinky / by Dave and Pat Sargent ; illustrated by Jane
Lenoir. — Prairie Grove, AR : Ozark Publishing, ©2001.
    ix, 36 p. : col. ill. ; 23 cm.   (Saddle-up series)

    "Don't be mischievous"—Cover.
    SUMMARY: In 1849, a mischievous sorrel horse proves
his worth when his owner and a friend, both prospectors, are
captured by outlaws who want to steal their gold nuggets.
Includes factual information on sorrel horses.
    ISBN: 1-56763-665-9   (hc)
          1-56763-666-7 (pbk)

    [1. Horses—Fiction. 2. Gold mines and mining—Fiction.
3. Frontier and pioneer life—Rocky Mountains—Fiction.
4. Robbers and outlaws—Fiction. 5. Rocky Mountains—
History—19th century—Fiction.]   I. Sargent, Pat, 1936- II.
Lenoir, Jane, 1950-   ill. III. Title. IV. Series.

    PZ10.3. S243Sr 2001
    [E]—dc21   2001-003043

Printed in the United States of America

iv

Inspired by

the beautiful reddish-brown sorrels
we see grazing beside the road.

Dedicated to

all who love beautiful sorrel horses.

Foreword

Stinky Sorrel belonged to an old prospector named Clem. Clem was busy searching for gold in 1849, when Stinky Sorrel, with the help of his three brand-new horse friends, capture three bad men. When Clem and his prospector friend, Seth, receive a reward, the two men and Stinky decide it's high time to head for California to grab their share of the gold nuggets that are supposedly just lying around on the ground. Now, don't forget the year, 1849. Could that be what is referred to as the California Gold Rush? Hmmm.

Contents

Stinky

If you would like to have the authors of the Saddle Up Series visit your school, free of charge, call 1-800-321-5671 or 1-800-960-3876.

One

Long-Handled Underwear

Early dawn cast light upon the majestic Rocky Mountains, literally unmasking the beauty of pine trees, rivers, and lakes. A wisp of smoke drifted upward from the chimney of a little cabin. The morning air was crisp and cold as Stinky walked to the front door and nickered softly.

"Come on now, Clem," he said. "Are you just going to sleep all day? It's time to get to work."

The door slowly opened, and a small man with a straggly white

1

beard stepped outside. He stretched and yawned before patting Stinky on the neck.

"I'm gonna prospect for gold nuggets today, big fellow," he said with a chuckle. "But I'm gonna wait until the weather warms up a mite."

The sorrel shook his head and pawed the ground.

"Okay, okay," Clem muttered as he turned back toward the cabin. "First, I'll have myself a big cup of coffee, and then we'll get to work. Maybe you're right, Stinky. We may find that big nugget this morning, and then we can both stop working."

"Humph," the sorrel grumbled. "Coffee tastes yuk. You should have a good ration of oats instead."

Hmmm. Speaking of oats, I'm going to try to find some while he's having his yukky cup of coffee. Stinky Sorrel smiled and nodded his head.

He trotted to a little shack behind the cabin and nudged the door open with his nose.

Several burlap bags were lined up against a wall amid the shovels, prospecting pans, and picks used for digging holes.

"Aha," he said. "My breakfast is in one of those bags."

He grabbed the first bag in his teeth. Then he dragged it from the shack before shaking the contents onto the ground.

"Hmmm," he groaned. "There is nothing but rocks in this one."

He picked up the second bag. A mouse had chewed a hole in the bottom of it, and oats poured out onto the floor. The sorrel smiled as he quickly backed out of the shack with the bag tightly clenched in his teeth. But by the time he found the right spot to enjoy his breakfast, the bag was empty. Glancing back toward the shack, he saw the trail of oats that began at the little building and ended at the empty burlap bag.

"Oops," Stinky mumbled as he started munching his way back toward the shack. "I better get this cleaned up before Clem sees it."

The sorrel horse had eaten half of the way back to the shack when he heard Clem shouting.

"Why, you ornery, mischievous stinker," he yelled. "Why didn't you just wait until I fed you? Now you've dumped out my fool's gold and you've wasted a bunch of oats!"

"No, I haven't, Boss," Stinky murmured. "If you'll just give me a little time, I'll clean up everything but the rocks. I'd eat the rocks, too, but they don't look very appetizing," he added with a chuckle.

Clem was madder than mad! He shook his fist high in the air! Then he reached down and grabbed the empty bag and swung it at Stinky. But the sorrel whirled and headed toward the big mountain, running as fast as his legs could go.

"Man alive," Stinky muttered. "I think I've really made him mad this time. He's never screamed at me like that before."

Stinky's ears were flat against his neck, and his eyes were tightly closed as he ran from the angry man. He kept glancing over his shoulder to see if Clem was gaining on him.

Good! He was outrunning him! Stinky glanced around to make sure, but only a moment later, he felt a rope against his chest, and his eyes popped open.

The old clothesline that held Clem's laundry as it dried was now stretched across Stinky's chest. As it tightened and broke, the man's long-handled underwear flew high in the air and fell over Stinky's head, neck, and back.

Again, he heard Clem's voice. This time it sounded scary!

"That does it, Stinky Sorrel! I'm going to town right now and trade you for a burro," Clem howled through clenched teeth. "Or I could just shoot you on the spot."

The scared sorrel shook the long-handles off his head and stared wide-eyed at his boss. The pitiful and painful vision of a burro eating his oats brought tears to his eyes. The terrible image was suddenly interrupted by a familiar voice.

"Howdy, Clem. How are you? I reckon you're getting ready to hunt for that big gold nugget again."

Stinky was relieved to see a friendly face, and he smiled as the short, stocky man walked up the path toward the cabin.

"I was, Seth, until Stinky pulled another one of his mischievous, ornery tricks on me," Clem growled. "I oughta take him back to the Rocking S Ranch where he came from, but I doubt if they want him."

Seth laughed and gathered up the rope and long-handled underwear. He tied the rope between two trees before hurrying toward Clem.

"Whew," Stinky sighed. "Now if he'll just clean up the oats, that burro may never get a bite of my breakfast."

"I have some good news and some bad news," Seth told Clem in a serious voice.

Clem raised one eyebrow and said, "Tell me the bad news first. That will make the good news sound even better."

"A gang of outlaws is robbing prospectors around here. They take all the money and gold they can find. They're a pretty mean bunch, Clem. Be on the lookout for them."

Suddenly the sorrel heard a strange noise. His ears shot forward. The sound of horses approaching prompted him to walk toward the tall pine trees west of the cabin. He nickered softly as a grey, a black, and a chestnut came into view. Then he noticed the men on their backs. Each man had his face covered with a bandanna, and they had their guns in their hands.

"Uh oh. This does not look good. They may be the outlaws that Seth was talking about," he gasped. "Oh boy! I don't even have time to warn Clem and Seth."

Two

The Bag of Fool's Gold

The sorrel glanced around for his prospector friends Clem and Seth. They were still at the shack. Clem had put the fool's gold back into the burlap bag, and the two men were on their knees, putting the spilled oats into a wooden bucket. Uh oh, the sorrel groaned. Neither of them have noticed the outlaws. He turned back toward the three approaching horses. Moments later, he greeted them before falling into step beside them.

"What are you doing here?" he asked the grey. "Your men do not look very friendly."

"They aren't," the grey replied. "They're going to steal your boss's gold."

"Yes," the chestnut replied. "They'll steal all his money and nuggets. I hate to see them tie up the men before tearing up their place to find it."

"Man alive! They are mean!" Stinky squealed. "I think you should just buck them off and find new bosses who are nice."

"Hmmm," the black mumbled. "That sounds like a good idea."

"I think so, too," the chestnut agreed.

Suddenly all three riders reined their horses to a halt. They aimed

19

their pistols at Clem and Seth before the man on the black horse spoke.

"Put your hands up and tell us where you hide all your gold," he growled in a deep, menacing voice.

Clem lunged for the man, but the outlaw shot the ground in front of the old prospector. Clem slowly backed away, and a moment later, both Clem and Seth raised their hands in the air.

"If you want it so bad," Clem said through clenched teeth, "find it. I won't show you where it is."

A good thirty minutes later, the outlaws were tearing up the cabin in search of the precious gold.

Clem and Seth were tied to a tree near the shack, groaning as they listened to the commotion taking place within the cabin.

Stinky Sorrel paced back and forth, trying to think of a plan to stop them. Suddenly he came to a halt, and his brown eyes glistened with anticipation. He quietly shared his plan with the black, the grey, and the chestnut before turning to Clem and Seth. His teeth gnawed on the ropes binding their hands. They were free!

Stinky raced to the front of the cabin and reared up on his hind legs. He nickered so loud that it sounded like a bellow from an angry bull.

"What's the matter with that horse?" a voice yelled from inside.

The sorrel kept squealing and bucking in a circle. He pawed the ground with his front hoof. And a moment later, all three outlaws were standing at the door watching him.

"He's loco," one of them said.

Again, Stinky shook his head and pawed the ground. He trotted to the path leading toward the shack, and then returned to the outlaws.

"He wants us to follow him," one said in a slow voice.

Stinky nodded his head and again trotted toward the path.

"He sure does," another agreed.

"Maybe he's taking us to the gold!"

Stinky pawed the ground and again nodded his head.

Stinky and the three outlaws raced past the tree where Clem and Seth had been tied. They were busy following the sorrel and didn't even notice the missing captives.

When Stinky reached the shack, he reached inside and picked up the bag of fool's gold with his teeth. The outlaws smiled as the golden rocks fell in a heap on the ground.

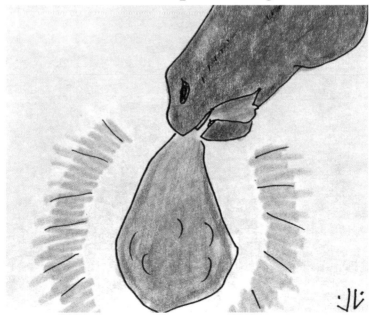

"Horse," one outlaw bellowed, "why don't you join our gang?"

"Humph," Stinky said. "I don't want to join your gang. You'll be on your way to jail soon, and I don't have any desire to be locked up."

Later, as the bandits mounted their horses, the sorrel whispered, "Okay, Grey, Black, and Chestnut, you know what to do now."

The three horses nodded their heads and winked at Stinky as the men settled down onto the saddles.

Three

Stinky Goes for the Gold

The three outlaws kicked their horses and reined them to the left. The big grey put his head down and started eating green grass. The black kicked with his back legs, but he did not move forward an inch. Then the chestnut suddenly lurched forward and hit a dead run before passing beneath the rope that held Clem's long-handled underwear. As the clothes wrapped around the rider, the reddish-brown horse began to buck. After several leaps into the air, his rider and the sack of fool's gold sailed over his head. The outlaw landed on the ground, and the Fool's Gold rained down on his prone body.

The grey suddenly grunted and began running in a big circle. When his rider tried to stop him, he whirled and ran straight toward a tree. And seconds later, his rider lay over a low-hanging branch kicking his legs.

The two prospectors got a drop on the third outlaw.

That evening after supper, Clem and Seth sat down on the porch. The outlaws had been delivered to the sheriff and the cabin was cleaned up, so the two friends were resting. Stinky dozed nearby as they talked quietly about the exciting day.

"That reward money will come in handy," Seth said with a chuckle. "We accidentally caught the outlaws and then got paid for it!"

"We didn't," Clem said gruffly. "Stinky and his three honest horse friends captured those bad outlaws. We just collected the reward."

Seth said, "I sure hope you've forgiven Stinky for his mischievous ways. You have, haven't you? As I recall, you were ready to send him back to the Rocking S Ranch or trade him for a burro this morning."

Clem glared at him before shaking his head. "Seth, there ain't enough gold in these hills to buy that horse of mine. That sorrel has earned his oats for a long time to come." He turned and looked at Stinky, who was grazing nearby.

The prospector said, "You said you had bad news and good news, but I never heard your good news. What is it, Seth?"

"California," Seth said in a loud voice. "Folks say there are big gold nuggets there just waiting to be picked up. I was thinking that you and I may go to California and get our share of the riches."

Clem slapped his leg and said, "I'm ready, Seth! We'll take off first thing in the morning." He got up and walked over to the sorrel.

"How does that sound to you, Stinky? Ready to go for the gold?"

Stinky smiled and nodded his head. Hmmm, he thought. If big gold nuggets are just lying on the ground waiting for us, I bet there are lots of folks running there to grab it. I wonder what they'll call this race for the gold nuggets? They could call it the California Gold Rush! The California Gold Rush of 1849. Oh, well, whatever they decide to call it, this mischievous sorrel horse is mighty proud to be a part of it. Yep! Life is great!

Four

Sorrel Facts

The sorrel is a light red horse. It is sometimes hard to distinguish between *sorrels* and *chestnuts*. Sometimes, it depends on the breed under consideration. Usually, if a horse has one or two shades of red or light color, it may be considered a *sorrel*.

In the American Quarter Horse breed the light, clear reds are always considered *sorrel*, regardless of the number of shades present. In any system that is used, the boundaries for the *sorrels* are very subtle, and some horses change shades during their lifetimes. Some people call the whole group of red horses "red" to avoid confusion.

Sorrels have clear red coats which combine with the various non-black point colors. Some *sorrels* have light manes and dark tails. Some have manes and tails that are lighter than the body.